The Wonderful Wedding

By Jean Waricha
Illustrated by S. I. Artists

A GOLDEN BOOK • NEW YORK

Golden Books Publishing Company, Inc., New York, New York 10106

Dear Barbie,

In three weeks I'm going to be the flower girl in my sister's wedding. I have a beautiful dress. I'm very excited, but I'm also a little nervous. Everyone will be watching me when I walk down the aisle. What if I make a mistake?

Love,

Jennifer

$\mathcal{B}$arbie sat down at her desk to answer Jennifer's letter. She wrote:

> Dear Jennifer,
>
> I'd like to tell you about the time my sister Stacie was a flower girl. She was nervous, too. Stacie was spending part of her summer vacation with me.

Barbie continued her letter to Jennifer. And this is the story she told. . . .

Barbie and her sister Stacie were having lunch when their cousin, Karen, rushed in. "I'm so excited!" she shouted. "Peter and I are getting married—and in just two weeks! Barbie, will you be my maid of honor?"

"I'd love to!" said Barbie.
"And will you be my flower girl, Stacie?" Karen asked.
"Oh, yes!" Stacie cried. "I can't wait to wear a fancy dress."
It was decided to have the wedding at Barbie's house.

The next morning, Barbie and Stacie went to the bridal shop.
Barbie selected a pink dress. "That is beautiful on you," said Stacie.

Then they looked at dresses for Stacie. "I think I've found it," said Barbie. "This is just the dress for a flower girl." Stacie was thrilled.

The next two weeks were so busy! Barbie helped Karen choose her dress, the cake, and the flowers.

The day before the wedding, Barbie set up the chairs while Stacie played with Seymour, her pet rabbit. But Barbie noticed that Stacie looked worried, so she asked her if anything was wrong. Stacie said she was afraid she might make a mistake.

"Don't worry," said Barbie. "We'll have a rehearsal."

On the day of the wedding, Barbie helped Karen and Stacie
get ready.

"I can't believe how beautiful we look," said Karen. "Barbie,
you're terrific with makeup and hairstyling."

Barbie even had a pink satin bow for Seymour.

Then Stacie took Seymour to the garden to wait for the guests.

"I'm going to check on the cake," Barbie told Stacie. "Try not to get your dress dirty."

Stacie decided to look in on Seymour, but when she opened the cage to pet him, he hopped out.

"Come back, Seymour!" cried Stacie.

Finally Stacie spotted Seymour under the hedge, but when she crawled in to catch him, her hair ribbon fell in the dirt. And when she pulled the rabbit out of the bushes, the bottom of her dress caught on a branch and tore.

As Stacie put Seymour back in his cage, she heard Barbie calling, "Stacie, the wedding's about to begin. Come get your flower basket."

Stacie hurried inside. "Oh, no!" she gasped. "I'm a mess!
I've got to find Barbie. She'll know what to do."

Stacie heard Barbie talking to Ken. She rushed to the window. "Barbie, please come up here right away," she called. "I need your help!"

Barbie found her sister in tears. "Seymour jumped out of his cage and I chased him," Stacie explained between sobs.

"Don't worry," said Barbie. "We'll figure something out."

Barbie took a beautiful shawl from her closet. "This will hide the spots," said Barbie. Then she pinned up the torn hem. "That looks beautiful," said Stacie, smiling.

"Now for the finishing touch," said Barbie, hurrying Stacie into the garden. Barbie picked some tiny pink roses and put them in Stacie's hair. "There," said Barbie—"you look perfect."

The wedding music began to play. Karen and Barbie watched proudly as Stacie scattered the flower petals down the aisle.

"Oh, Barbie," said Karen, "thanks to you and Stacie, this is truly the most wonderful wedding!"

Barbie smiled as she finished her letter:

And so, Jennifer, if something goes wrong at your sister's wedding, don't worry. Just have fun. Your sister will be happy, knowing that you were there to share her special day.

Love,

Barbie